RAPUNZEL

AN EROTIC FAIRYTALE

CLOVER'S FANTASY ADVENTURES
BOOK 8

VICTORIA RUSH

VOLUME 8

CLOVER'S FANTASY ADVENTURES -
BOOK 8

COPYRIGHT

ALSO BY VICTORIA RUSH

Adult Fairytales:

The Enchanted Forest: An Erotic Fairytale

The Land of Giants: An Erotic Fairytale

The Dragon's Lair: An Erotic Fairytale

Witch's Brew: An Erotic Fairytale

The Mage's Spell: An Erotic Fairytale

The Mermaid Lagoon: An Erotic Fairytale

The Coven: An Erotic Fairytale

Rapunzel: An Erotic Fairytale

The Seven Dwarfs: An Erotic Fairytale

The Land of Mutants: An Erotic Fairytale

The Erotic Temple: A Sexy Fairytale (Coming Soon)

Erotica Themed Bundles:

Voyeur: Lesbian Erotica Bundle

Public Affairs: A Lesbian Anthology

Futa Fantasies: The Ladyboy Collection

Threesomes: The Lesbian Collection

Threesomes - Volume 2: The Lesbian Collection

First Time: A Lesbian Anthology

Hedonism: An Erotic Anthology

Switch Hitters: Bisexual Erotica

Taboo Erotica: The Lesbian Series

BDSM: The Lesbian Collection

Party Games: The Erotic Collection

Party Games 2: The Erotic Collection

All Girl 1: Lesbian Erotica Bundle

All Girl 2: Lesbian Erotica Bundle

All Girl 3: Lesbian Erotica Bundle

All Girl 4: Lesbian Erotica Bundle

Erotic Fairytale Bundles:

Clover's Fantasy Adventures: Books 1 - 5

Clover's Fantasy Adventures: Books 6 - 10

Erotic Fantasy:

Pirate's Bounty: A Time Travel Adventure

Wild West: A Time Travel Adventure

Private Riley: A Time Travel Adventure

Cleopatra's Secret: A Time Travel Adventure

Bounty Hunter 2125: A Time Travel Adventure

Ninja Assassin: A Time Travel Adventure

The 300: A Time Travel Adventure

Arabian Nights: An Erotic Fairytale (coming soon...)

Steamy Time Travel Bundles:

Riley's Time Travel Adventures: Books 1 - 5

Lesbian Erotica:

The Dinner Party: Lesbian Voyeur Erotica

The Darkroom: Bisexual Voyeur Erotica

Naked Yoga: Lesbian Transgender Erotica

Nude Cruise: Bisexual Voyeur Erotica

Rush Hour: Taboo Public Sex

The Girl Next Door: First Time Lesbian Erotic Romance

Girls' Camp: Lesbian Group Sex

Wet Dream: Ladyboy Fantasy Erotica

The Convent: Taboo Sex with a Nun

Sex Robot: A Dream Sex Machine

The Personal Trainer: Getting Pumped at the Gym

The Dominatrix: BDSM Lesbian Domination

Webcam Chat: Lesbian Online Sex

Paint Me: A Kinky Bodypainting Workshop

The Toy Party: Girls Sharing Sex Toys

The Costume Party: Strapping One On

Swedish Sauna: Lesbian Group Sex

The Therapist: Taboo Lesbian Erotica

Elevator Shaft: Bisexual Threesomes Erotica

Ladyboy: Lesbian Transgender Erotica

Peep Show: Lesbian Voyeur Erotica

The Dare: Public Sex Erotica

Maid Service: Lesbian Threesomes Erotica

The Hitchhiker: First Time Lesbian Erotica

The Housesitter: Spycam Lesbian Erotica

The Spa: Lesbian Group Orgy

Parlor Games: Blindfold Sex Party

The Exchange Student: First Time Lesbian Erotica

The Hostel: Bisexual Group Erotica

The Harem: Lesbian Erotic Romance

The Orient Express: Lesbian Voyeur Erotica

The First Lady: A Forbidden Lesbian Erotic Romance

The Slave: Lesbian BDSM Erotica

The Masseuse: Lesbian Sensuous Erotica

Too Close for Comfort: Lesbian Forbidden Erotica

Naked Twister: A Wild Party Game

Lexi: The Sex App (Lesbian Fantasy Erotica)

Call Girl: Lesbian Bisexual Threesomes Erotica

Circle Jill: Lesbian Masturbation Workshop

The Viewing Room: Masturbation Voyeur Erotica

Spin the Bottle: A Kinky Party Game

The Hair Salon: Lesbian Voyeur Erotica

Tribadism 1: Girls Only Sex Workshop

Tribadism 2: The Art of Scissoring

Tribadism 3: Threeway Hookups

The Kiss: A Game of Oral Sex

Pledge Week: Sorority Sisters

Carny Games 1: A Wild Sex Party

Carny Games 2: A Kinky Sex Party

Carny Games 3: An Erotic Sex Party

Dreamscape: An Artificial Reality Game

Glory Hole: Guess Who's On the Other Side

Joy Ride: A Late Night Erotic Bus Trip

The Blind Girl: An Erotic Romance(Coming Soon)

Lesbian Erotica Bundles:

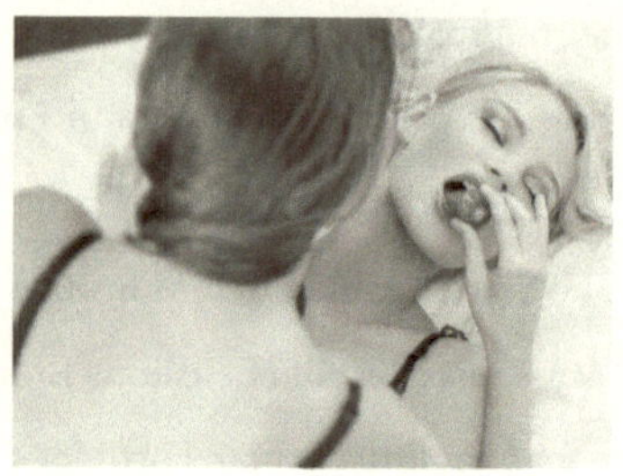

Jade's Erotic Adventures: Books 1 - 5

Jade's Erotic Adventures: Books 6 - 10

Jade's Erotic Adventures: Books 11 - 15

Jade's Erotic Adventures: Books 16 - 20

Jade's Erotic Adventures: Books 21 - 25

Jade's Erotic Adventures: Books 26 - 30

Jade's Erotic Adventures: Books 31 - 35

Jade's Erotic Adventures: Books 36 - 40

Jade's Erotic Adventures: Books 41 - 45

Jade's Erotic Adventures: Books 46 - 50

Fifty Shades of Jade: Superbundle

Standalone Stories:

The Polynesian Girl: A Lesbian EroticRomance

WANT TO AMP UP YOUR SEX LIFE?

Sign up for my newsletter to receive more free books and other steamy stuff. Discover a hundred different ways to wet your whistle!

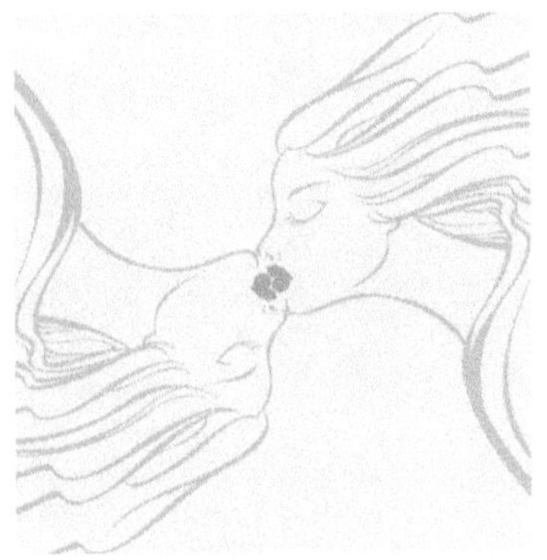

Victoria Rush Erotica

1

After Clover's harrowing escape from the witches' coven, she and her friends headed deeper into the forest in search of some food.

"Man, I'm starved after being cooped up in that cave for so long," Jessop said, peering through the bush for any sign of wild game.

"Yeah," Tara grunted. "Food wasn't exactly the top priority of our recent hosts."

"I think you're being generous referring to those witches as *hosts*," Clover nodded. "At least they won't be terrorizing any more innocent travelers for a while, now that they're trapped in their little torture chamber."

"It wasn't *all* bad," Jessop smiled, pointing toward a boar digging for some roots in a thicket. "Where else can we enjoy unrestricted sex with a bunch of strangers on an improvised stage?"

"If you don't mind being burned alive after you get your rocks off," Tara chuckled, pulling an arrow out of her quiver.

She placed the arrow on her bowstring and pulled it back, aiming at the unsuspecting animal. When she released the dart, it impaled the boar on its flanks, and it squealed in pain until Clover closed the distance, slicing its throat to put it out of its misery.

"At least we have the decency to kill our quarry before roasting it for dinner," Clover nodded, beginning to skin the animal while Jessop and Tara prepared the fire.

"So what now?" Jessop said while the group sat around the fire to enjoy their braised pork.

"I guess we just follow our noses," Tara said, tearing into the succulent meat. "We always seem to find a new adventure around the next corner."

Clover stared into the fire pit, watching the sparks dancing in the air.

"I don't know about you guys," she said. "But I could use a little rest and relaxation after our last escapade. Maybe we should lay low for a little while."

"Works for me," Tara nodded, laying out her bedroll to begin turning in for the night.

The next morning, the trio headed further inland, hoping to escape the bustle of the towns and villages closer to the sea. After a few hours, they noticed a tall tower standing next to a farmhouse, and they crouched lower in the brush, peering at one another curiously.

"What's that?" Jessop said, squinting his eyes at the strange-looking object. "Some kind of granary?"

"I don't know," Tara said, examining the structure more carefully. "It doesn't seem to have any kind of entrance or exit other than the small window near the top."

"Maybe it's some kind of watchtower to protect the people living in the cottage," Clover said, noticing a narrow tendril of smoke swirling above the lone chimney on the side of the cabin.

"That's a pretty tall watchtower for such a modest house," Jessop said, scanning the surrounding area for any other sign of activity.

"I think we should continue on our way," Tara nodded, rising up and motioning for her friends to follow. "Whatever it is, it looks sturdy enough to resist any intruders from trespassing on their territory. Remember what we said about keeping a low profile for a while–"

"Wait," Jessop said, tilting his head toward the top of the tower, noticing a glimmer of light reflecting off the window. "There's somebody in there."

While the friends knelt back down in the bushes, they noticed a girl looking to be in her late teens opening the window and tumbling her long hair over the edge of the sill.

"Oh!" Jessop gasped, catching his breath at the sight of the pretty girl.

Her coppery-red hair glistened in the morning sunlight, stretching down almost the full length of her body. Her face was pale, but her emerald eyes sparkled like jewels, and when she stretched her arms lazily outside the window, Jessop could see the curvature of her plump breasts pressing against her thin nightgown.

"That's a strange place for a *bedroom*," he said, mesmerized by the sight of the seductive maiden.

"So much for it being a watchtower," Tara nodded, peering inside the chamber for any other sign of occupation. "She looks to be all alone up there."

"It wouldn't hurt to say hello," Jessop said, turning toward his friends with a hopeful expression. "She doesn't seem to be any kind of threat to us..."

"That's what we thought when we stumbled upon the

witches' coven," Clover said. "Appearances can be deceiving. Besides, she doesn't appear to be in any kind of distress–"

Suddenly, the girl thrust a wooden bucket outside her window, flinging a cascade of dirty water down the side of the tower.

"Unless you count having to piss in a bucket and being cooped up in a brick tower with no visible means of escape," Jessop said, adjusting his crotch while he gazed up at the golden-haired beauty. "Why don't we see if she's being held against her will..."

"I don't know," Clover said, darting her eyes over the girl's voluptuous figure. "She seems well enough fed..."

"Let's see if anyone else is home," Jessop said, peering toward the cottage. "Something doesn't feel right here."

Clover turned toward Tara, and the elf simply shrugged her shoulders.

"It wouldn't hurt to check it out," she nodded.

"Okay," Clover said, glancing at Jessop. "But keep your eyes peeled for any sign of trouble. The last thing we need is to be led into another ambush."

As the trio crept toward the cottage, they huddled close to the walls, peering inside one of the windows. The house appeared to be starkly furnished, with a lone pot resting on the wood stove and a single place setting laid out on the small kitchen table.

"Whoever lives here," Tara nodded, peering around the spartan interior. "They seem to lead a modest life. It looks like only one person lives here."

"*Two*, if you count the girl in the tower," Jessop said, noticing a box-sized opening in the adjoining wall. "It looks like the only access to the tower is via the dumbwaiter on the side wall."

"Yes," Clover said, furrowing her brows at the unusual arrangement. "It appears that she's locked in the tower with her only connection to the outside world being the food elevator and her small outside window."

Jessop pulled himself away from the wall, heading back in the direction of the tower.

"Let's go talk to her to find out what's going on," he said.

"Jessop," Clover said, grabbing his shirtsleeve to slow his

progress. "Maybe we should leave well enough alone. We only get ourselves into more trouble whenever we poke our noses into other people's business."

"Maybe so," Jessop said, pulling his arm away. "But look at all the people we've helped along the way. The lonely princess in the land of giants, the Amazon women on the island of Sappho, the slaves in the witches' coven. Besides, there doesn't appear to be anyone else home right now to stop us."

"Okay," Clover sighed, nodding toward Tara. "But only for a few minutes. We have no idea when the owner of the house will return."

The group circled around to the opposite side of the tower, then they peered up toward the high window, noticing the golden-haired girl had retreated back inside and closed the window panes. Jessop searched the ground for some small stones, then he stepped back a few paces, throwing the pebbles gently toward the glass. The stones tinkled off the panes, and after a few seconds, the window angled outward once again, and the maiden poked her head through the opening, glancing down. When she saw the trio standing at the base of her tower, she gasped in surprise, taking a step backward.

"Wait!" Jessop called up to her. "We don't mean you any harm. What is your name?"

"Rapunzel," the girl said, poking her head slowly through the window.

"Do you live here alone?" Jessop said. "I mean in the tower. Do you have any way out of there?"

"No," the girl said. "My mother lives alone in the cottage, but I'm being locked up in the tower under orders from the prince."

"What prince?" Jessop said. "We didn't see any castles in the vicinity..."

"Prince Garibald," Rapunzel said. "His castle is half a day's ride from here. After I was betrothed to him, he insisted that I be locked in this tower until our wedding day to protect my virtue against any unwanted suitors."

"Is this something you *agreed* to?" Jessop said, peering at the maiden with a puzzled expression. "This seems highly unusual..."

"Definitely not," the girl said. "He met me in the woods while his entourage was on a fox hunt, and he claimed me upon first sighting. But I was too young at the time for marriage, so he had this tower built while my mother watched over me."

"How long ago was that?" Jessop said, noticing her long tresses spilling over the windowsill.

"I've been locked up here for almost five years."

"Five years!" Jessop said. "All alone in this tower with no contact with the outside world?"

"Not unless you count the daily feedings sent up to my room by my mother or the periodic visits by the prince."

"Do you have any other way out of there?"

"No," the girl said. "My only portal to the outside world is through this narrow window. And it's far too high to scale down the outside walls."

Jessop scanned the masonry of the exterior wall, running his hand over the narrow cracks between the bricks.

"Would you leave if you could do so?" he said.

"In a heartbeat," Rapunzel nodded. "My mother's only interested in the dowry she'll receive once I'm bequeathed, and the sight of the prince turns my stomach whenever I see him."

Jessop paused while he turned toward Tara and Clover, tilting his head beseechingly.

"It can't be that hard to save one more damsel in distress," he smiled.

"Are you sure you only have *her* interests at heart this time?" Clover said, noticing the bulge in the crotch of his trousers.

"Whatever secondary benefits we might gain from saving her are incidental," he grinned. "We've never hesitated to save other individuals in similar circumstances. The fact that she just happens to be sexy and gorgeous is irrelevant. We can't leave her up there to be ravaged by some over-bearing prince."

"Mm-hmm," Clover hummed, curling up one side of her mouth. "What do you think, Tara? Are you willing to go out on a limb one more time?"

Tara paused for a moment while she peered at her two friends.

"She seems old enough to make her own decisions," she nodded. "Maybe if we leave a note for her mother so she won't worry about what happened to her..."

"Alright then," Jessop said, peering back up toward the girl in the tower. "But how are we ever going to scale this structure?"

Clover and Tara glanced at the walls of the tower, then they looked up at the narrow opening a hundred feet above the ground.

"I don't think it's a matter of us going *up* there so much as her coming *down*," Tara said, lifting her bow off her shoulder. "If I connect some fishing line to the end of an arrow and fire it inside her window, she can use that to haul up a heavier line to climb down with."

"What exactly did you have in mind?" Clover said,

peering around the grounds for some extra rope. "We didn't exactly come prepared for this kind of extraction."

"Why don't you guys search inside the cottage for something?" Tara said. "Maybe we can tie a bunch of curtains together to make an improvised ladder. I'm sure her mother can get by with one or two fewer comforts after the deprivations she's subjected her daughter to these past few years."

Jessop nodded then he peered up toward Rapunzel, who was gazing down at them with a bewildered expression.

"Hold still for a few moments longer," he called up to her. "We're going to send you a lifeline in a few minutes."

"Okay," the girl said. "But you better hurry. I don't know when my mother will return from foraging in the forest, and the prince could make another unannounced visit any time now. If he catches you trying to rescue me, he'll have your heads."

"Don't worry, sweetheart," Jessop grinned, noticing the girl's nipples darting the front of her nightgown. "This isn't the first time we've battled superior odds to save someone in distress. Have you got something a little more comfortable to wear for traveling clothes?"

"Nothing that fits me," Rapunzel said. "I'm afraid I've outgrown most of my other clothes."

"I guess we'll just have to make do then," Jessop said, winking at Clover while they headed toward the cottage.

3

———

Tara tied the reel of her fishing line to the end of one of her arrows, then she peered up the tower toward Rapunzel.

"Stand to the side of the window," she said, pulling her bowstring back. "I'm going to fire an arrow into your cabin, then you can pull a thicker cord up."

Rapunzel stepped away from the window, and Tara shot her arrow through the opening just as Clover and Jessop returned with a handful of curtains.

"I'm not sure if this will be enough to reach all the way to the top, but it was everything we could find," Jessop said, handing the material to Tara.

"Help me tie the pieces together with double knots," she nodded, tying the end of one curtain to the end of her reel.

After all the parts were connected, she glanced back up toward the tower window, where Rapunzel was peering down at them with excitement.

"Okay," Tara called up. "Pull the clothesline up to your window, then tie one end securely to something heavy in your room."

The three friends watched the quilted rope inch its way up the wall, then Rapunzel disappeared inside her chamber to tie off one end. When she returned, the opposite end rested forty feet off the ground.

"Now what?" Clover said. "There's no way she'll be able to jump the remaining distance without hurting herself."

"You couldn't find anything else in the cabin?" Tara said.

"No," Clover said. "We even stripped the sheets off the bed. There wasn't a lot to work with."

Tara peered back up toward the window, noticing the girl staring down at them with a confused expression.

"Can you tie your bed linens to the other end of the line?" the elf called up. "It's not long enough to reach the bottom."

The girl disappeared inside her room and after a few minutes, the friends noticed the makeshift cord sliding back down the wall. But when Rapunzel reappeared at the window, the end of the line still rested twenty feet above the surface of the ground.

"Is that everything you've got?" Tara said.

"Everything besides my nightgown," Rapunzel nodded.

Tara turned toward Clover and Jessop, cocking her head.

"What do you guys think?" she said. "Will it work?"

"I don't think there's any other way," Jessop said, already imagining the sexy girl climbing down the rope in the nude.

"Assuming that flimsy nightgown will even support her weight," Clover nodded.

"It might if she ties it to the end nearest the ground," Tara said. "That way, if it breaks, at least she'll have a shorter distance to fall. Maybe we can build some kind of safety net to catch her."

"That could work," Clover nodded.

"Works for me," Jessop grinned.

"Alright," Tara said, nodding up toward the girl. "We just need a little more length of rope. Can you pull the line back up and connect your nightgown to the end closest to the ground? We'll catch you if it's still not long enough."

"Are you sure?" the girl said, wrinkling her forehead as she peered down toward the ground.

"We're going to make something soft for you to land on," Tara nodded.

"Ok," the girl said, pulling the line back up toward her window. After a few minutes, she threw the cord back outside the portal, with her cotton nightgown flapping ten feet above the ground.

While Clover and Tara collected some loose pine boughs in the forest, Jessop raced inside the cabin to grab the mattress off the bed, then they piled everything into a thick pile at the base of the tower.

"Okay," Tara said, calling back up to the girl. "This is as good as it's going to get. Do you feel strong enough to climb down the rope?"

"I'll give it a try," the girl said, pushing one leg over the edge of the sill while clutching the tufted line tightly in her hands.

"Cross your legs around the rope to help support your weight," Tara called up, trying to ease the girl's fears.

"And grab the knots for a more secure handhold," Clover nodded.

"Can you wrap your hair around your shoulders to keep it out of the way?" Jessop added, more interested in seeing her naked body than trying to be helpful.

While they watched Rapunzel angle her body out the window, her long hair still fell halfway down her back, partly covering her exposed buttocks. But as she slowly crept down the line while flexing her legs to absorb her weight, it was impossible not to notice the golden bush and dark slit between her thighs.

"Are you *enjoying* this?" Tara said to Jessop, noticing him craning his head upward as his eyes bulged wide as saucers.

"I'm just preparing to catch her if she falls," he said, moving closer to the base of the tower.

"That's not the *only* thing you look like you're getting ready to do," Clover chuckled, noticing the bulge in his pants.

But when the girl reached the end of the line, she clutched onto the end of her nightgown, dangling her legs nervously over the bed of prickly pine branches.

"It's okay," Jessop said, trying not to stare at her glistening pussy. "You can let go and I'll catch you."

But as she dangled at the end of the line, unwilling to let go, suddenly a hail of arrows darted around them, and the group twisted around, watching four horses emerge from the edge of the forest.

"Stop, in the name of the king!" a man in a puffy hat and silk robes called out, flanked by two guards and a flagbearer. "That girl belongs to me."

Rapunzel turned her head around, and her eyes opened wide when she recognized the man on the horse.

"It's Prince Garibald!" she said as her nightgown suddenly tore apart and she fell headlong into Jessop's arms, collapsing in a heap atop the prickly pine boughs.

4

"I'm afraid the girl feels otherwise," Tara said to the prince, stepping in front of Rapunzel and stretching her bow tightly as she pointed an arrow toward the entourage.

"She doesn't have any choice in the matter," Garibald said, flaring his eyes at the girl's naked body when she stood up, brushing the pine needles off her skin. "She's been promised to me upon the king's orders."

"She's not a piece of *property* you can buy and use at your leisure," Jessop huffed, standing next to Rapunzel.

"We'll have to see about that," the prince said, motioning for his guards to approach the group standing at the base of the tower.

"Halt, or we'll have to defend ourselves," Tara said, pulling her bowstring back tighter.

"Do you three think you're any match against the king's guard?" the prince scoffed, darting his eyes over the motley trio.

"I suppose we're about to find out," Tara said, aiming her

arrow at a patch of unprotected flesh under one of the guard's padded sleeves.

The guards checked their horses, peering toward the prince for further instructions.

"What are you waiting for?" he said, glaring at them impatiently. "Attack!"

The horsemen galloped toward the group and Tara felled the first guard with her arrow while Clover snapped her bullwhip around the second guard's neck, pulling him off his horse. Then they quickly closed the distance, grabbing each of the men behind their necks and pointing their daggers toward their throats. The prince stared at them dumbfounded for a moment, then he motioned for his flagbearer to lower his lance and charge toward Jessop and the girl. Jessop positioned Rapunzel behind his back then he charged toward the horse, dropping onto his knees and slicing the horse's ankle, causing it to rear up onto its hind legs, throwing the flagbearer onto the ground while Jessop pointed the tip of his sword onto his neck.

"Fancy yourself a swordsman, do you?" the prince said, sliding off the side of his horse and drawing his saber. "Let's see how you do against a properly trained *fencer*."

The prince lowered himself into an attack position and Jessop lifted his sword from his opponent's throat and spread his legs apart, placing his free hand on his hip. When the prince lunged toward him with his sword raised over his head, Jessop blocked it as their swords clanked together in a flash of polished steel. Within a few seconds, Jessop had the prince stumbling backwards until he was pinned against the side of a tree with his saber falling out of his grasp. He leaned in toward the prince and clutched his throat while pressing the end of his sword against his belly under his breastplate.

"Not so tough without your bodyguards to protect, are you?" he sneered as the prince winced in pain.

"Jessop!" Clover said, disarming the other soldiers while Tara kept an arrow trained on the group. "We didn't come here to kill anybody. They're no longer a threat to us without their weapons. Let him go and we'll continue on our way. We've already rescued the girl."

Jessop paused as he stared at the prince, pinching his airway.

"Why don't we at least take their *horses*?" he said. "That way we'll be able to put some extra distance between us before he orders more of his lackeys to chase after us."

"If the castle is a half day's ride away, that will give us plenty of time to evade them," Clover said. "Besides, we don't have enough provisions to take care of four horses."

Jessop sneered at the prince for a moment, then he pushed him aside.

"You better forget your claims on the girl," he said. "She has no interest in you, and there's no way we're going to let her be locked up again."

The prince glanced at his attendants then he angled his head toward the forest.

"Mount up," he said. "I'll decide what to do with you clowns when we return to the palace. This floozy isn't worth the effort anyway. As for the rest of you, I wouldn't get too comfortable traipsing around these woods. We have spies everywhere."

After the group disappeared into the forest, Rapunzel flung her arms around Jessop, clutching him tightly.

"Thank you for saving me!" she gushed. "I didn't think anybody could stand up to the prince."

"There was only a *few* of them this time," Tara said, wrapping her bedroll around Rapunzel's naked body. "But I have a feeling this isn't the last we've heard of the prince. Do you have somewhere else you can go?"

"No," the girl said, shivering from a combination of fright and chill. "After my father died in a hunting accident, my mother was the only one left to look after me."

"You can stay with us at least until we find a safer place for you to hole up," Clover nodded. "Are you hungry?"

"Yes," Rapunzel said. "I haven't eaten for almost twenty-four hours."

"We'll build a camp in the woods and catch some game for dinner," Tara said, glancing at the girl's long tresses covering her naked ankles. "And get you some proper clothes."

"You can huddle next to me in the meantime," Jessop smiled, wrapping his arm around her shoulder to keep her warm.

"Yes," Rapunzel said. "I feel safer next to you anyway."

"Let's go, you lovebirds," Tara said, rolling her eyes. "The more distance we can put between ourselves and that randy prince, the better."

5

Rapunzel and her new friends headed in the opposite direction of the castle, then they made camp while Tara and Jessop foraged for some dinner. When they returned, Jessop dragged a twelve-point stag behind him, then they skinned the animal, hanging its hide next to the fire while Clover dressed the meat.

"I'll stitch together some clothing for you after the hide dries," Tara said, motioning toward the deerskin.

"And you can use my bedroll to stay warm tonight," Jessop said, adding some logs to the fire.

"With or without you lying beside her?" Clover smiled, handing everyone a drumstick of roasted venison.

"I'm guessing the last thing Rapunzel wants right now is another man forcing himself upon her," Jessop said.

"It will actually be nice to have some company for a change," the girl said. "It's been pretty lonely up there in that tower all by myself these past few years."

"I can imagine," Tara nodded, scanning her curvy figure wrapped up in the blanket. "At least you seem to have been well fed during that time."

"Not with anything as delicious as this," Rapunzel said, tearing into her drumstick with dripping lips.

"Maybe it just tastes better now that you have your freedom," Clover said.

"Thank you again," Rapunzel said, peering around the group. "For rescuing me from the tower and fighting off the prince. You took a tremendous risk taking on his entire entourage."

"The odds were pretty even this time," Tara said. "But if he comes back with a larger army, we'll have to be more careful to evade his hunting party."

"Yes," Clover nodded. "It's probably best that we stay away from the towns and villages for a while. Nothing will be more obvious than a girl with long hair, a Westerner, and an elf traveling with a youth."

"I can take care of myself," Jessop huffed. "I'm no longer a child."

"I didn't suggest you were," Clover said. "But if the prince has put a bounty on our heads and a posted reward for finding Rapunzel, we just need to keep a low profile until we get a little further away."

"I didn't mean to cause you any trouble..." Rapunzel said.

"It's not your fault," Tara said, reaching out to clasp the girl's hand. "It was our choice to rescue you."

"You must be tired after all the excitement of the day," Jessop said, getting up to prepare the camp for the night. "We should rest before setting out on the next leg of our journey."

After everyone finished dinner, Jessop hung the deer carcass from a tall tree branch a few hundred feet from their camp, then the four travelers laid out their bedrolls around the fire, turning in for the night. For the next half hour or so, everything was quiet and still while the campfire crackled and cast shadows over the surrounding woods. But after a short while, Rapunzel heard the sound of a snapping twig in the forest, and she rolled over next to Jessop, clutching him closely.

"What was that?" she said, peering into his eyes.

"Probably just a wild animal picking up the scent of the deer," Jessop said, feeling her breasts pressed up against his chest.

"Are we safe lying next to the fire?" Rapunzel said. "What if it's a band of wolves or a bear?"

"The fire should keep them away from us," Jessop nodded, pulling her closer. "Don't worry, I'll keep you safe."

"What if it's the prince returning with another group of soldiers?" Rapunzel said, looking at Jessop with a worried expression.

"Do you want me to check it out?" he said, feeling his cock thickening as Rapunzel rubbed her naked body against him.

"Would you mind?" she said.

"Of course not. You just stay here and keep warm."

Jessop reluctantly pulled himself from under the blanket, then he unsheathed his sword, creeping slowly in the direction of the sound from the forest. After a few minutes, he saw two orange eyes peering up at him from behind a small bush, and he shooed the animal away with a swish of his blade. Scanning the area to make sure there was no other threat, he returned to the girl's bedroll, nestling in next to her.

"What was it?" she said, shivering next to him.

"Just a raccoon," Jessop said. "I scared him away and we should be safe for the rest of the night."

"Can I sleep next to you?" Rapunzel said, pressing her body closer to Jessop. "I'm not used to being alone outside at night."

"Of course," Jessop said, feeling his cock swelling against his pants while he held the naked girl.

"What's that bulge in your pants?" the girl said, rubbing her hand over his crotch. "Are you hurt?"

"No," Jessop chuckled. "That's just my penis getting excited about having a naked woman lying next to me."

"Is that what happens when a man and a woman lie next to one another?"

"You really *have* been locked up for a long time, haven't you?" Jessop said. "Didn't your parents teach you about the facts of life?"

"I suppose they thought that was the prince's job after we got married."

"That's one way to find out about sex," Jessop laughed.

"Can you *teach* me?" Rapunzel said, rubbing her hips against Jessop. "I've never been with a man like that before."

Jessop hesitated while his mind raced with a thousand possibilities.

"Have you never even touched yourself to give you pleasure?" he said, reaching under his waistband to straighten out his aching member.

"Yes, but I have no idea how it works when you're with someone else."

"Well it kind of works the same way," Jessop said, grinding his hips against Rapunzel's soft bush. "It feels just as good for the man when he rubs his sex organ. Even *better* when he does it with a partner."

"Is *this* how you like to rub it?" the girl said, stroking his hard-on over his tightening pants.

"Kind of," he grunted. "Only usually without any clothes on."

"Mmm," Rapunzel said, unclasping his belt. "I want to see what a man feels like down there..."

"Ungh," Jessop groaned when his erection popped out of his pants.

"It's so big!" Rapunzel gushed, curling her fingers around his shaft. "And *hard*."

"Eh," Jessop shuddered as she began to slide her fist up and down his pole. "Not much bigger than most, I imagine."

"Does it feel good when I touch it like this?"

"Very," Jessop panted.

"Tell me what *else* you like," Rapunzel said, stroking his erection awkwardly.

"Well it's more fun when we rub our sexy parts *together*," Jessop said, pressing his fingers between Rapunzel's thighs and feeling her wet vulva. "That's why I have an outtie and you have an innie. Our organs were designed to be joined together. That's how babies are made."

"Is *that* where they come from?" Rapunzel said, rolling her thumb over Jessop's dripping crown.

"You've got to be kidding me," Jessop said, hardly believing the sheltered girl was so naive.

"Unfortunately not," Rapunzel said. "I've been locked up by myself and there are no schools so deep in the forest."

"Well, yes," Jessop said, slipping two fingers into Rapunzel's slit while massaging her clit with his thumb. "When a man and women join together, the man ejects a seed into the woman's womb, which eventually grows into a baby."

"Is that what all this sticky stuff is that's coming out the end of your penis?"

"Yes," Jessop groaned as Rapunzel rolled her fingers over his throbbing crown. "Although a lot more comes out when we reach the pinnacle of pleasure."

"Show me," Rapunzel said, spreading her legs further apart. "I want you to take me to the pinnacle of pleasure and feel you plant your seed inside me."

"I don't think either one of us is ready to have a baby right now," Jessop nodded. "But maybe it won't hurt to press it inside for a short while."

"Yes," Rapunzel mewed, rolling onto her back as she spread her knees wide apart. "I want to experience pleasure when somebody else is touching me. Put your big penis inside my hole and let's experience pleasure together..."

"Are you sure?" Jessop said, reluctant to take advantage of the innocent girl. "I don't want to force myself upon you–"

"You're not forcing me to do anything," Rapunzel said. "We're just doing what a man and a woman are designed to do. I want to feel your sex inside me."

"Okay," Jessop said, rolling over atop the girl. "But technically that part of my body is called a *cock* when it's hard. I suppose we should be using the anatomically correct terms if we're going to do this."

"Yes," Rapunzel said, grabbing the tip of his organ and pointing it toward her opening. "Put your cock inside my hole. Let's make pleasure together."

"Oh God," Jessop moaned when he felt the tip of his organ enter her slippery slit. "Your pussy feels so warm."

"Is that the anatomically correct name for my baby hole?" Rapunzel said, placing her hands over the back of Jessop's buttocks and pulling him deeper inside her.

"Yes," Jessop chuckled, thrusting his dick deep inside her

cavity.

"Mmm," Rapunzel moaned. "I like the feeling of your cock inside my pussy. This feels even better than when I rub my pleasure button by myself."

"That's called your *clitoris*, but I don't suppose we need to worry about what we call those parts right now."

"No," Rapunzel grunted, beginning to roll her hips rhythmically with Jessop as their pleasure began to mount. "Just slide your cock inside my pussy and make us throb together. I can feel it starting to tingle like it does when I touch myself."

Jessop smiled at Rapunzel's use of awkward terms to describe their sex act, and he lowered his mouth onto hers as much to stifle her rising moans as to lose himself in her pleasure. But when he heard her moans becoming louder and more urgent, he began to feel the familiar pangs of an impending orgasm building in his balls. Fearful of impregnating her with his semen, he pulled out of her just as she groaned in ecstasy, jerking her body in orgasmic convulsions while he spurted his cum all over her belly.

"Oh my God," she groaned, rubbing her fingers through his sticky spunk. "Is that what your baby seed feels like?"

"Yes," Jessop chuckled. "But it's called *semen*, or come, or...never mind. Did it feel good for you too?"

"Oh yes," Rapunzel said, squeezing Jessop's throbbing cock in her fist. "Can we do it again?"

"Maybe a bit later," he grunted. "Men need a little more time to recover after having sex than a woman."

"That's too bad," she said. "Because I'm starting to like this business of making sex together."

"Well, there's more than one way to give a woman pleasure during sex," he smiled, drifting his mouth over Rapunzel's neck and across her hard nipples.

6

———

In the morning, the group enjoyed quail eggs and boar bacon around the fire while Clover and Tara eyed Jessop and Rapunzel suspiciously.

"Did you sleep well last night?" Clover said, noticing the flush in Rapunzel's cheeks.

"Best I have in a long time," she nodded.

"Must be the fresh air," Jessop said.

"Or the excitement from escaping the tower," Tara said.

"It was a pretty exciting day all around," Clover nodded, smiling knowingly at Jessop.

"So what's our plan for today?" Jessop said, trying to change the subject. "Moving further away from the castle?"

"I think we should head into town to stock up on provisions," Tara said. "I need some needle and thread to make clothes for Rapunzel, and maybe we can find a map of the surrounding area to help navigate our route. We're kind of operating in the blind in this territory and we need every advantage we can find to stay out of the prince's clutches."

"What about our plans to keep a low profile?" Jessop said. "I thought you said it wasn't safe to go into town?"

"Not if two of us go," she said. "They'll be looking for three travelers and a girl with long hair. If only you and I go, hopefully we won't arouse any suspicion."

"Okay," Jessop nodded. "But who'll look after Rapunzel if the prince finds our camp? Clover won't be able to fend them off all by herself."

"Don't worry about us," Clover said. "I'll build a blind in one of the trees and remove the traces of the fire. The deer carcass should distract them from our location while we wait it out."

"Alright," Tara said, slinging her bow over her shoulder and ruffling her hair to conceal her pointy ears. "We shouldn't be more than a few hours. Whistle twice when you see us return. Are you ready to go, Jessop?"

Jessop paused while he attached his sword to the side of his belt.

"Are you sure we should be bringing our weapons?" he said. "They'll be looking for a girl with a bow and a man with a sword. If we're only going to the general store, we shouldn't need any protection."

"Maybe you're right," Tara nodded, handing Clover her bow and quiver of arrows. "Clover could use them better than us anyhow. We'll be back soon enough."

After Tara and Jessop headed in the direction of the nearest settlement, Clover set to work cleaning up the camp and building a shelter in a nearby tree. While she shimmied up the tree, she used her bullwhip to shuttle up broken branches and pieces of vine, using thin strips of bark to fasten everything together to create an improvised sling. When she finished creating their hideaway, she lowered her whip from the tree, motioning for Rapunzel to climb up. After some effort, the girl managed to shimmy up the rope, then the two women carefully climbed the branches to lower themselves in the sling.

"Are you alright?" Clover said, noticing Rapunzel grimacing while she caressed the inside of her thighs.

"I think so," the girl said, peering at the welts on her skin. "It's just a bit of chafing from climbing the rope."

Clover pressed her knees further apart and gently slid her fingers over the scratches, nodding her head.

"They'll heal up in a couple of days," she said. "We'll get some proper protection on you after Tara returns with some needle and thread."

Rapunzel peered over the edge of the swing, glancing at the long distance to the ground.

"I didn't think I'd have to be so high up again after you freed me from the tower. I was kind of getting used to having my feet on the ground."

"It shouldn't be for long," Clover said. "Just until evening to stay out of sight of the prince's hunting party."

"Do you think he'll come back so quickly?"

"That kind of man doesn't give up so easily," Clover nodded. "I think we hurt his pride more than anything else. Now he's got a chip on his shoulder and something to prove."

Rapunzel leaned against Clover, placing her head on her shoulders.

"Well, I feel safe with you," she said. "And I don't mind being trapped above ground when I've got some friendly company. Where are you from?"

"I come from a land very far away, called America," Clover said.

"I've never heard of such a place," Rapunzel said.

"Neither has anyone else," Clover chuckled. "It's a bit of a long story how I got here."

"How did you meet Tara and Jessop?"

"Tara saved me from a pack of wolves after I landed in Abbynthia, and Jessop came to our rescue when an evil warlock tried to ambush us."

"You three seem to make a habit of saving damsels in distress," Rapunzel laughed.

"Maybe so," Clover smiled, wrapping her arms around Rapunzel to keep her warm. "They seem to make a habit of crossing our paths."

"Is Jessop yours and Tara's sex partner?" Rapunzel said. "You all seem to be very close."

"When the mood strikes us," Clover chuckled, laughing at Rapunzel's straightforward manner. "But it's just a union of convenience. We try not to let romance get in the way of our survival strategies."

"So you're not planning on making babies together?" Rapunzel said, stroking Clover's crotch over her sheepskin bodysuit.

"God no," Clover said, spreading her knees apart unconsciously. "That's the last thing we need right now. We barely manage to escape one adventure after another without a helpless child in tow."

"Can Tara make babies too? She seems different from the two of you..."

"I would imagine so," Clover nodded, feeling her pussy beginning to dampen as Rapunzel continued caressing her vulva. "She's equipped with the same parts as the rest of us. Only her ears are shaped a little differently."

"So she's got a pussy like you and me?" Rapunzel said.

"Yes," Clover grunted, becoming increasingly aroused by Rapunzel's tickling of her crotch.

"And it feels good to touch it like this?"

"Yes–and in *other* ways." Clover said.

"Can you show me how?" Rapunzel said. "Jessop showed me how a *man* touches a woman's sex last night, but I've never tried it with a woman."

"It's not so different," Clover said, slipping her hand under Rapunzel's long tresses and between her thighs. "If two people are sufficiently aroused, all it takes is a little friction in the right places."

"Using your hands?" Rapunzel said, rolling her hips sexily while Clover caressed her dripping pussy.

"And other body parts."

"Show me," Rapunzel said, spreading her knees wider apart. "I want to learn everything about having sex with other people."

"I suppose it wouldn't hurt to amuse ourselves while we wait for Tara and Jessop to return," Clover smiled. "Let me move into a more comfortable position where we can enjoy this more easily."

She raised her body up and pulled off her bodysuit, then she positioned herself on the other side of the sling, facing Rapunzel with their hips facing one another. When Rapunzel sliced her legs apart, Clover threaded her thighs between her knees, pressing their pussies together in a scissor position.

"Huh!" Rapunzel gasped when she felt their vulvas joining together.

"You see," Clover grinned. "Any two people can enjoy sex together with the proper motivation and technique. Sometimes even *three* or more..."

"You mean as a group?" Rapunzel said, widening her eyes.

"Mm-hmm," Clover nodded, grinding her hips against

Rapunzel. "Perhaps we'll show you when we have some more free time."

"Mmm," Rapunzel purred, clasping the side of Clover's buttocks and pulling her harder toward her cunt. "I like it this way. But Jessop said only a man and a woman were meant to be joined together like this."

"You must have misunderstood him," Clover said. "He certainly enjoys it plenty enough when he watches Tara and I have sex together."

"Does that mean you don't need an innie and an outtie to make sex between two people?"

Clover smiled at Rapunzel's charming innocence. She found the combination of her voluptuous figure and her naivety all the more alluring.

"Well, it doesn't hurt to have a hard cock in the mix every now and then," she chuckled. "But you tell *me*, does this feel as good as when you and Jessop had sex last night?"

"You heard us?" Rapunzel said, suddenly flaring her eyes open. "I thought you were sleeping."

"It was pretty hard to sleep with the two of you moaning and grunting all night. Not to mention all the funny questions you were asking."

"I'm sorry if I seem so uneducated," Rapunzel said. "It's just that I've never had sex with another person before last night."

"It's quite alright," Clover said. "I rather enjoyed listening to the two of you. I got just as turned on as you did and had a climax around the same time you did."

"What's a climax?"

"The feeling you get when you reach the peak of your pleasure and your body involuntarily pulses and shakes. Do you feel like you're getting closer to having one this way?"

"Yes," Rapunzel panted, tilting her body sideways to

grind her clit against Clover's. "It feels even *better* with all this extra lubrication."

"Better than with a cock inside you?" Clover smiled.

"Just different," Rapunzel groaned. "I like being able to see the look on your face when I'm giving you pleasure."

"You're giving me plenty of pleasure right now," Clover grunted, feeling her orgasm rapidly approaching while Rapunzel's long hair brushed over the side of her hips. "You're going to make me come soon..."

"Is that the same thing as a climax?" Rapunzel said, grasping Clover's ass with both hands while she humped their pussies together.

"Yes," Clover panted. "Come with me, Rapunzel. You're so beautiful..."

"Mmm," Rapunzel mewed as a flush began to spread over her chest. "I can feel it now. I'm going to come so hard with you..."

Suddenly, the two women began squealing while they shook their hips together, watching each other's faces flushing and their mouths gaping open while they convulsed their bodies together in ecstatic union. After they finished coming for what seemed like a full minute, they relaxed their bodies, collapsing back onto their respective ends of the hammock.

"Wow," Rapunzel said, panting heavily. "That might have been even better than the sex I had with Jessop."

"And it's three *times* as pleasurable when we all doing it together," Clover smiled.

"You mean *four*," Rapunzel smiled, already looking forward to expanding her carnal education with her sexy new friends.

7

While Clover and Rapunzel were getting to know one another better, Tara and Jessop made their way to the nearest village. When they reached the end of town, they scanned the main street for any sign of the prince's retinue, then they headed toward the General Store. When the doorbell clanged to signal their entrance, the proprietor looked up, scanning the young customers suspiciously.

"What can I help you with?" he said, running his eyes over Tara's animal hide bodysuit.

"Do you have some needle and thread?" she asked.

"Of course," the man nodded, reaching behind the counter. "Did you have a particular color in mind?"

"Something neutral like white will do," Tara said.

The man placed a roll of thread on the counter then peered up.

"Will one spool be enough?" he said.

"I better take two," Tara smiled. "You know, just for emergencies."

"Of course," the proprietor said. "You can never have

enough thread around the house."

"Mm-hmm," Tara nodded, scanning the store shelves for a map.

"Is there something else I can get for you?" the man said, noticing Jessop keeping a close watch by the window.

"Do you have a map of the area?" Tara asked.

"You're not from around here, then?"

"Just passing through," Tara said.

The man pulled a folded map from a side shelf and placed it on the counter next to the needle and thread. Tara unfolded it and bent over the chart, looking for the location of the prince's castle and its proximity to their location in the forest.

"Looking for anything in particular?" he said, raising his eyebrows when he noticed Tara's pointed ears poking out from her fallen hair.

"Not really," Tara said, folding up the map and placing it under her arm together with the needle and spool of thread. "How much do we owe you for all this?"

"That'll be three shillings," the man said, angling his head toward the young couple when a burly man suddenly entered the front door.

"Keep the change," Jessop said, slapping a gold coin on the counter.

"Leaving so soon?" the burly man said, grabbing Tara's wrist tightly.

Jessop glanced up at the proprietor and withdrew his hand just before a sharp dagger slapped down over the counter, narrowly missing his fingers. Tara pivoted her body in the direction of the heavy-set man, grabbing his palm with her free hand and bending his arm awkwardly backward, kicking him as hard as she could in his balls, then pulling the knife out of the counter and slicing his throat cleanly. When the proprietor attempted to reach under the counter for another weapon, she spread her legs wide apart, holding his knife by the tip of its blade, arched threateningly over her shoulder.

"Don't even *think* about it," Tara said to the man. "Unless you want to end up like your accomplice. I know how to handle these things, and I'm not afraid to use it."

The man raised his hands slowly in the air and backed away from the counter, then Tara and Jessop peered out the front window to make sure the way was clear.

"And don't bother notifying the sheriff," Tara nodded, sidestepping the pool of blood rapidly spreading around the fallen man's body. "Unless you want to make more of a mess of your pretty little store."

The man nodded his head nervously then the two friends exited the store quickly, disappearing down a side alley and rushing into the safety of the surrounding forest.

When they returned to the location of their camp, Clover and Rapunzel were nowhere to be found, and they scanned the treetops, looking for any sign of their hiding place. When they didn't see anything, Tara whistled twice then two more whistles wafted from a nearby tree. Tara and Jessop peered up, and Clover dropped a small pebble to signal their location.

"What took you so long?" she said, climbing down from the tree with Rapunzel to join her friends on the ground.

"We ran into a little glitch at the store," Tara said. "I think the proprietor recognized us. We better get out of here while the getting is still good. I'm pretty sure the prince's spies will have passed the word along regarding our location by now."

"Okay, but which way?" Clover said, noticing the map under Tara's arm.

Tara knelt down on the ground and unfolded the map,

pointing to their location and the location of the prince's castle.

"Maybe we can lose them in mountains," she said, tracing her finger toward a brown ridge in the west. "Plus we'll have the advantage of the high ground to scan the area and hopefully see them coming so they don't surprise us next time."

"Sounds good," Clover nodded, handing Jessop and Tara their weapons. "But what about stitching Rapunzel's clothing? She's getting pretty banged up traipsing around with only her long hair to cover her."

"It'll have to wait until we find a safer hideout," Tara said, slinging her bow over her back and peering toward Jessop. "Can you fetch the deer hide hanging from the other tree? It should be dry by now."

"Of course," Jessop said, running into the brush to retrieve the hide.

While he was briefly separated from the group, Tara glanced at Rapunzel, recognizing a flush on her cheeks and some scratches on the inside of her thighs.

"Are you good to go?" Tara said, noticing her erect nipples poking through the long strands of curly red hair falling over her plump breasts.

"Absolutely," the girl nodded excitedly. "I haven't had this much fun in ages. I'm ready to go wherever you want to take me."

"Alright," Tara said, throwing a blanket over her shoulders. "Try to stay close and not trip over your hair. We might have to cut some of that off later so you don't stick out like a sore thumb."

"No worries," Rapunzel smiled, glancing at Jessop's bulging crotch after he returned. "I'll stick close as glue. And we can worry about things that stick out later."

8

For the next three hours, the group traveled through the forest toward the mountains in the west. When they arrived at the escarpment, they climbed the slope until they reached a tall bluff overlooking the sea. The sun was beginning to set and the view from the cliff was breathtaking as the sea glimmered in the darkening light.

"It looks like this is as far as we can go in this direction," Jessop said, resting wearily on a fallen log.

"Let's hope the prince doesn't plan on going this far," Tara nodded, pulling her bow and quiver off her back.

"If he does, our exit options will be limited," Clover said, peering over the edge of the sheer cliff dropping thousands of feet to the forest floor.

"It wouldn't hurt to rest for a while," Jessop said, his cock beginning to twitch again at the thought of bedding down next to Rapunzel.

"Maybe just for a day or two," Tara nodded, preparing a campfire next to the cliff. "For the time being, I think we should focus on catching some food for dinner."

While the three friends disappeared into the forest to

find some wild game, Rapunzel gazed out over the darkening sea, falling asleep from exhaustion after the long hike. When she awoke, she saw Tara sitting at the edge of the blazing fire stitching the deer hide while Clover turned a pig carcass on the spit and Jessop added some extra logs to the fire.

"Mmm," she hummed, sniffing the scent of the roast pig. "That smells good. I'm starved after our long hike in the woods."

"Well, try not to eat *too* much," Tara smiled, peering at her naked figure. "I've fashioned this bodysuit to match Clover's size, but I have a feeling it will be a little more snug on your curvy figure."

"I like the idea of wearing clothes to match yours," Rapunzel nodded, sitting up. "It makes me feel like I'm part of the clan. I'm growing more attached to the three of you with every passing day."

"Come," Tara said, holding up the garment. "Let's see how it fits."

Rapunzel stood up and stepped into the short leg holes, then she turned around while Tara pulled her hair to the side and threaded up the back panels, forcing the girl's breasts to lift and squeeze together.

"It's *snug* alright," Rapunzel said, raising her knees one at a time to test its flexibility. "But I kind of like the feeling of the soft fabric hugging my naked body."

"I like the *look* of the fabric hugging your body," Jessop chuckled, adjusting his crotch in his tightening pants while he stared at the bottom of Rapunzel's butt cheeks poking out the bottom of her cut-off leggings.

"How do I go *pee* in this thing?" Rapunzel said, spreading her hands over the front of the animal hide.

"That's one of the shortcomings of wearing a one-piece

suit," Clover nodded. "You've got to take the whole thing off whenever you have to do your business. But the advantage is that there's fewer seams to tear and fall apart. My suit has survived pretty much intact for the six months since Tara stitched it together."

"I *like* it," Rapunzel smiled, wrapping her arms around her three friends and pulling them closer. "Now we're all in this together."

~

After the group finished dinner, a chill began to drift in from the sea and they laid out their bedrolls to turn in for the night. But once again, Rapunzel was the odd person out without a blanket to lie on, and Jessop rolled over to offer up his space.

"Why don't we all sleep together tonight?" Rapunzel said. "We'll have more blankets to cover us, and we can share our body warmth like the wolves do when they sleep in their animal dens.

"It's not a bad idea," Tara said, peering at Clover and Jessop, who nodded eagerly. "It will also keep us between the fire and the open escarpment to protect us against any encroaching animals while we sleep."

"Okay then," Rapunzel said, patting the two halves of Jessop's blanket as she lay sexily on her side. "Come lie with me while we warm each other up."

The three friends moved over to Rapunzel's blanket and as they snuggled together, Rapunzel pulled the other blankets over their bodies.

"Mmm," she purred. "This is much better. Even better than rubbing my body next to Clover or Jessop."

"Well, I'm glad *I* finally get a turn," Tara chuckled, planting her face in Rapunzel's cleavage.

"Clover said the two of you like to have sex occasionally," Rapunzel said, threading her knee between Tara's legs.

"*Did* she now?" Tara smiled, rolling her hips against Rapunzel's thigh.

"And that Jessop likes to watch sometimes." Rapunzel nodded.

"Sometimes," Jessop said, shifting over to create a tight sandwich between their four figures. "But it's even more fun to *participate* in the action."

"How do you do that with two women at the same time?" Rapunzel said, pinching her eyebrows together. "With only one cock and two pussies?"

"You'd be surprised how versatile three people can be when they're properly motivated," Jessop smiled, rolling on top of the three girls and grinding his cock against their undulating asses.

"What about with *four* people?" Rapunzel said. "I've been dreaming about rubbing against *all* of you ever since I slept with Jessop and Clover."

"Well, the first order of business is for each of us to get *naked*," Tara smiled, raising up and taking off her body suit. "Then we can worry about where to connect all the fun parts."

"Mmm," Rapunzel hummed, twisting around while Tara unstrung her back panel.

It didn't take long for Clover and Jessop to follow suit, and within seconds everybody was lying naked next to one another and rolling around on the blanket, rubbing their crotches against any open flesh they could find.

"This is good," Tara said, rolling onto her back while pulling Rapunzel next to her. "But we need a bit more direct *friction* if everyone's going to enjoy this equally. Why don't you and Clover face one another while you sit on top of me and Jessop moves behind us to have his choice of the litter?"

"Okay," Rapunzel said, wrinkling her forehead, still unsure how to position herself. "Where do you want me to sit exactly?"

"On my face," Tara smiled, pulling Rapunzel's hips over her head and spreading her knees apart. "That way you and Clover can play with each other's tits while you rub your pussies on my body and Jessop fucks us from behind."

"Oh my God," Rapunzel squealed, tossing the top blanket aside. "Now I see what you mean about liking to *watch*. This way I can see all of us having sex together."

"And *I* get to watch you fucking Tara's face while I pound her ass," Jessop grinned, pulling Tara's knees up toward her hips while he stared at Clover's and Tara's pussies joined together.

"Or *mine*," Clover smiled, grinding her slippery mound over Tara's.

"Or *both* of ours," Tara nodded.

"One at a time, ladies," Jessop nodded, inserting his throbbing organ into Tara's dripping hole while he clenched his fingers around Clover's ass.

"*Fuck* yes," Tara grunted when she felt Clover's clit sliding over her button as Jessop fucked her with his thick prick. She placed her hands over the inside of Rapunzel's thighs and spread her knees wider apart, lowering the girl's dripping pussy onto her lips, sucking her erect gland hard into her mouth.

"*Oh God,*" Rapunzel gasped. "That feels so good. Suck my pussy with your pretty face, Tara. Just when I thought this couldn't get any better..."

"Mmm," Clover said, leaning forward to thrust her

tongue into Rapunzel's mouth while she squeezed her tits and rocked her body over Tara's mound as Jessop fucked her from behind. "We might have to make you a permanent addition to our group if you keep this up."

"Yes, please," Rapunzel smiled, grinding her pussy harder against Tara's flapping tongue.

"Aren't you forgetting something?" Clover said, turning her head toward Jessop. "You've got two pussies to choose from back there. Don't forget to share the love."

"You're twisting my arm, babe," Jessop smiled, pulling his glistening cock out of Tara's hole and driving it into Clover's cunt.

"Ungh," Tara groaned, rolling her tongue over Rapunzel's hardening clit. "I can feel your balls slapping against my pussy while you fuck Clover. I'm going to cum soon..."

"No fair!" Rapunzel said, peering at the look of ecstasy on Jessop's face as his balls began to tighten around the base of his cock. "You girls get to have his cock all to yourselves while I only get to look at his *face.*"

"She's got a point, J," Tara chuckled. "Why don't you slide it between our pussies so we can *all* watch your pretty dick while we rub our bodies together?"

"I like the sound of that," Jessop said, pulling out of Clover's hole and placing his erection in the crevasse between their two vulvas while they ground their slits together. As he thrust his hips forward and back, the three women peered down, noticing his purple head poking out between their rocking hips while he spread precum all over Tara's undulating belly.

"Yes, baby," Tara grunted. "Shoot your load all over my stomach while we watch you get off."

"Fuck yes," Jessop grunted, squeezing Clover's ass tighter with the tips of his fingers while he watched Rapunzel's gaping mouth as she neared her own orgasm. "I'm going to come hard. The three of you look so amazing together."

"Oh God," Clover suddenly gasped, arching her back and tilting her head backwards. "I'm going to come all over your balls. Your cock feels so hot between Tara's and my cunt. Here it comes–"

Suddenly, a thick jet of fluid shot out between the two women's pussies, and when Jessop felt Clover squirting over his balls, his dick began pulsing in powerful contractions, jetting his semen high up over Tara's stomach, coating her tits and nipples while she squeezed Clover's breasts in the throes of orgasm. While all four lovers howled in delirious ecstasy, little did they know that far below them in the forest below, the prince was advancing toward their position with a pack of tracking dogs and an entire regiment of the king's soldiers.

9

———

At the crack of dawn, the group was awoken by the sound of barking dogs, and Jessop threw off their blanket, peering over the edge of the escarpment.

"What is it?" Clover said, rubbing the sleep out of her eyes.

"It's the prince," Jessop said, furrowing his forehead. "And he's brought a much larger army with him this time."

"Have we got enough time to escape?" Tara said, sitting up with alarm.

"I don't think so," Jessop said. "He's separating his troops into three parts to cut off all our exits from the escarpment."

"With a sheer cliff behind us, we'll be trapped," Clover nodded.

"What are we going to do?" Rapunzel said, peering at the others with frightened eyes. "I don't want to fall into the prince's clutches again. There's no telling what he'll do to me after I tried to escape."

"Not to mention the *rest* of us," Jessop said. "I'm afraid this doesn't look good. It seems that our strategy of hiding out in the mountains has backfired. Now we've got nowhere else to go."

Clover paused as she peered around the campsite and out toward the open sea.

"Maybe not," she said. "How much time have we got before the soldiers reach our position?"

"Maybe an hour at best," Jessop said.

"I've got an idea," Clover nodded. "But we'll have to work fast. We've got enough materials to build a kite to fly away to safety."

"Fly?" Tara said, looking at Clover like she'd lost her marbles. "With *what*? We don't exactly have wings."

"Well, technically, we'd be *gliding*, not flying. And we wouldn't be using wings–it would be more like a parachute."

"What's a parachute?" Jessop said, shaking his head in confusion.

"It's a device used to slow your fall when you jump out of an airplane–" Clover began. "Never mind. Just trust me on this. I've seen it done back where I come from. And it works."

She began looking around the clearing, searching for the necessary supplies.

"We're going to need four sturdy poles about ten feet long each and three shorter branches about three feet long. Plus a sling that will support our combined weight."

"I'll begin chopping the poles," Jessop nodded, pulling out his knife.

"And I can stitch the sling," Tara said, gathering up the blankets.

"I need you to work on the *canopy*," Clover said to Tara. "Three blankets should be enough. Just remember to use double stitching over the seams. We'll have to use our body-suits to create the sling."

Clover began to collect their clothing lying on the ground then she peered over at Rapunzel.

"I'm sorry, Rapunzel, but we're going to have to ask you to go naked for a little longer. We're going to need every stitch of clothing we can find to make this apparatus work."

"No problem," Rapunzel smiled. "I'm happy to get naked with you whenever you need me. Just tell me what you want me to do."

"I need you to tie the ends of the garments together with the tightest knots you can make, just like we did with the bed sheets to escape from your tower. In the meantime, I'm going to cut some strips of bark to begin making some twine to hold everything together..."

As the four friends set to work building the pieces of the glider, they listened to the sound of the dogs in the distance gradually growing closer. Within thirty minutes, all the parts lay on the ground, and the group peered at Clover, wondering what to do next.

"What now?" Tara said, pinching her eyebrows together. "How does this *parachute* thing work?"

"We need to make a large triangle," Clover nodded, kneeling down onto the dirt to tie each end of the long poles into a pyramid shape using the bark twine. "Then we're going to cover it with the blankets, which will create a type of airfoil."

As the group stood over Clover, watching her attach each of the pieces, they shook their heads in confusion.

"How are we going to *steer* this contraption, assuming it will even fly?" Jessop said.

Clover tied the ends of the smaller branches into a U-shape, then she attached the bar to the front end of the glider, connecting the two ends of the tied bodysuits to the lateral edges of the glider.

"We're going to use our *bodyweight*," Clover nodded, flipping the delta-shaped kite over and raising it over her head as the wind rising over the escarpment billowed the sails. "At least that's the way it should work in theory."

"You mean you've never actually *flown* one of these things?" Tara said, looking at Clover incredulously.

"No," Clover said. "But I've seen it done in the movies."

"The *what*?" Jessop said.

"Look," Clover said, peering at her friends impatiently. "You're just going to have to trust me on this. Assuming the seams have been stitched together tight enough and the blankets don't tear, it should be strong enough to support all of us–"

"That's a lot of assumptions to make such a giant leap of faith," Tara said, shaking her head doubtfully.

"We can always take our chances with the *prince* if that's what you'd prefer," Clover said, listening to the sound of horses' hooves and barking dogs nearing their camp.

"Alright," Tara said, nodding toward the others. "Just tell us what to do. Let's get the hell out of here while we still can."

10

———

As the group tried to wedge their bodies onto the sling, Clover shook her head, struggling to control the yoke in the swirling wind.

"There's not enough room for us to sit four-abreast," she said, motioning for the others to step off. "Jessop will have to sit beside me while you two sit on our laps. Then we'll push off using our legs and I'll do the steering."

"Okay," Tara said, grabbing her bow and arrows before they stepped into the improvised sling. "I sure as hell hope this thing works."

As soon as everyone had taken position, the prince emerged from the edge of the thicket, flanked by a company of mounted soldiers and a team of attendants holding four snarling dogs on the ends of tight leashes.

"Well, well, well," he sneered when he saw the naked group sitting awkwardly on the glider sling. "What do we have here? It looks like you've grown a little more comfortable with each other while I've been away."

"Don't come any closer," Tara huffed, facing the prince

with her legs wrapped around Clover's waist while she pointed an arrow at the soldiers.

"Or *what*?" the prince chuckled. "You'll only be able to drop one of my men before my hounds tear you apart."

"I only need to drop *one* of them," Tara scowled. "I'm only aiming at you."

"You don't actually think you can escape from me again?" the prince laughed. "We've got you surrounded on every side with nowhere else to go."

"I wouldn't be so sure about that," Tara said, tapping Clover's hip with her knee to signal it was time to go. "You underestimated us before, and we've got a secret weapon this time."

"You mean that dragon-shaped contraption?" the prince scoffed. "You don't actually think it will *fly*, do you?"

"It doesn't need to fly," Clover said, motioning for Jessop to begin running toward the edge of the cliff. "It only needs to glide..."

When they began running toward the side of the cliff, the prince motioned for his men to release the dogs, and as they raced toward the tangled quartet, everybody's eyes widened as they moved closer toward the precipice. When they fell over the cliff, the kite suddenly angled downward, dropping below the embankment just as a torrent of arrows shot over their heads.

"Eeee!" Rapunzel screamed in fear, feeling the group falling toward the forest floor while the others flared their eyes wide open in terror.

Remembering what she'd seen in the documentary about hang-gliding, Clover pushed the steering bar forward with all her might, and the group's weight slowly moved backward on the kite, lifting the front of it upward. While they rushed toward the approaching treetops at near terminal velocity, suddenly the wind filled their canopy, and the kite began to arc upward, skimming over the top of the branches as their feet flapped through the leaves. Within seconds, they were swooping through the air, angling from side to side while Clover steered the bar to the left and the right.

"Oh my God!" Tara exclaimed, watching the shocked look of the prince and his entourage fade away while they raced away from the cliff. "You had me going for a minute there. I wasn't sure this thing was going to work."

"When have I ever steered you wrong before?" Clover smiled, pressing her tits against Tara's while the two of them clamped their legs together for support on the rocking sling.

"You mean besides the encounter with the evil warlock, the shape-shifting witch, and the blood-thirsty band of pirates?" Tara chuckled.

"But I managed to get you out of each of those pinches, didn't I?" Clover said, tilting her hips forward to rub their pussies together.

"Perhaps not with quite the same degree of panache," Tara smiled, kissing Clover hard on her lips.

"So where are we going to now?" Rapunzel said, watching the treetops swooshing below them as they rode a current of air down toward the sea.

"Well, this thing has to land *somewhere*," Clover said, scanning the distant shore. "And I have a feeling the beach will be a little softer to land on than these prickly pine trees."

"Don't rush on my account," Jessop grunted, humping his hips against Rapunzel's criss-crossed thighs while the girl's eyes began to glaze over.

"I wouldn't get too comfortable over there," Clover

chuckled. "I don't want you to break something just when it looks like we're finally in the clear."

"I dunno," Jessop grinned. "I kind of *like* having sex while we suspended in the air."

"Welcome to the *mile-high-club*," Clover chuckled, feeling her own pleasure beginning to build while Tara humped her vulva with her slippery mound.

"The what?" Jessop said.

"Never mind," Clover smiled, watching Rapunzel's long hair flapping in the wind while it brushed over their bodies. "Just enjoy the view while you have the chance."

Ready for more erotic chills and thrills? Order the next exciting volume in Clover's Fantasy Adventures, *The Seven Dwarfs*. Buy direct and save at *victoriarusherotica*. Or download from your favorite online bookstore here: *retailer links*.

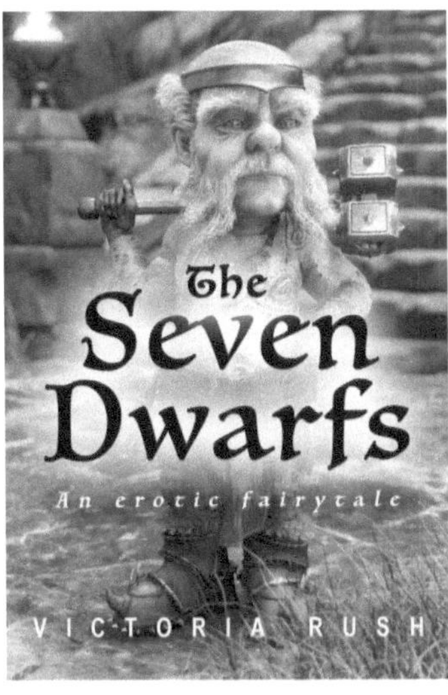

Seven randy dwarfs. Three unsuspecting visitors. A hundred sexy combinations...

ALSO BY VICTORIA RUSH

Adult Fairytales:

The Enchanted Forest: An Erotic Fairytale

The Land of Giants: An Erotic Fairytale

The Dragon's Lair: An Erotic Fairytale

Witch's Brew: An Erotic Fairytale

The Mage's Spell: An Erotic Fairytale

The Mermaid Lagoon: An Erotic Fairytale

The Coven: An Erotic Fairytale

Rapunzel: An Erotic Fairytale

The Seven Dwarfs: An Erotic Fairytale

The Land of Mutants: An Erotic Fairytale

The Erotic Temple: A Sexy Fairytale (Coming Soon)

Erotica Themed Bundles:

Voyeur: Lesbian Erotica Bundle

Public Affairs: A Lesbian Anthology

Futa Fantasies: The Ladyboy Collection

Threesomes: The Lesbian Collection

Threesomes - Volume 2: The Lesbian Collection

First Time: A Lesbian Anthology

Hedonism: An Erotic Anthology

Switch Hitters: Bisexual Erotica

Taboo Erotica: The Lesbian Series

BDSM: The Lesbian Collection

Party Games: The Erotic Collection

Party Games 2: The Erotic Collection

All Girl 1: Lesbian Erotica Bundle

All Girl 2: Lesbian Erotica Bundle

All Girl 3: Lesbian Erotica Bundle

All Girl 4: Lesbian Erotica Bundle

Erotic Fairytale Bundles:

Clover's Fantasy Adventures: Books 1 - 5

Clover's Fantasy Adventures: Books 6 - 10

Erotic Fantasy:

Pirate's Bounty: A Time Travel Adventure

Wild West: A Time Travel Adventure

Private Riley: A Time Travel Adventure

Cleopatra's Secret: A Time Travel Adventure

Bounty Hunter 2125: A Time Travel Adventure

Ninja Assassin: A Time Travel Adventure

The 300: A Time Travel Adventure

Arabian Nights: An Erotic Fairytale (coming soon…)

Steamy Time Travel Bundles:

Riley's Time Travel Adventures: Books 1 - 5

Lesbian Erotica:

The Dinner Party: Lesbian Voyeur Erotica

The Darkroom: Bisexual Voyeur Erotica

Naked Yoga: Lesbian Transgender Erotica

Nude Cruise: Bisexual Voyeur Erotica

Rush Hour: Taboo Public Sex

The Girl Next Door: First Time Lesbian Erotic Romance

Girls' Camp: Lesbian Group Sex

Wet Dream: Ladyboy Fantasy Erotica

The Convent: Taboo Sex with a Nun

Sex Robot: A Dream Sex Machine

The Personal Trainer: Getting Pumped at the Gym

The Dominatrix: BDSM Lesbian Domination

Webcam Chat: Lesbian Online Sex

Paint Me: A Kinky Bodypainting Workshop

The Toy Party: Girls Sharing Sex Toys

The Costume Party: Strapping One On

Swedish Sauna: Lesbian Group Sex

The Therapist: Taboo Lesbian Erotica

Elevator Shaft: Bisexual Threesomes Erotica

Ladyboy: Lesbian Transgender Erotica

Peep Show: Lesbian Voyeur Erotica

The Dare: Public Sex Erotica

Maid Service: Lesbian Threesomes Erotica

The Hitchhiker: First Time Lesbian Erotica

The Housesitter: Spycam Lesbian Erotica

The Spa: Lesbian Group Orgy

Parlor Games: Blindfold Sex Party

The Exchange Student: First Time Lesbian Erotica

The Hostel: Bisexual Group Erotica

The Harem: Lesbian Erotic Romance

The Orient Express: Lesbian Voyeur Erotica

The First Lady: A Forbidden Lesbian Erotic Romance

The Slave: Lesbian BDSM Erotica

The Masseuse: Lesbian Sensuous Erotica

Too Close for Comfort: Lesbian Forbidden Erotica

Naked Twister: A Wild Party Game

Lexi: The Sex App (Lesbian Fantasy Erotica)

Call Girl: Lesbian Bisexual Threesomes Erotica

Circle Jill: Lesbian Masturbation Workshop

The Viewing Room: Masturbation Voyeur Erotica

Spin the Bottle: A Kinky Party Game

The Hair Salon: Lesbian Voyeur Erotica

Tribadism 1: Girls Only Sex Workshop

Tribadism 2: The Art of Scissoring

Tribadism 3: Threeway Hookups

The Kiss: A Game of Oral Sex

Pledge Week: Sorority Sisters

Carny Games 1: A Wild Sex Party

Carny Games 2: A Kinky Sex Party

Carny Games 3: An Erotic Sex Party

Dreamscape: An Artificial Reality Game

Glory Hole: Guess Who's On the Other Side

Joy Ride: A Late Night Erotic Bus Trip

The Blind Girl: An Erotic Romance(Coming Soon)

Lesbian Erotica Bundles:

Jade's Erotic Adventures: Books 1 - 5

Jade's Erotic Adventures: Books 6 - 10

Jade's Erotic Adventures: Books 11 - 15

Jade's Erotic Adventures: Books 16 - 20

Jade's Erotic Adventures: Books 21 - 25

Jade's Erotic Adventures: Books 26 - 30

Jade's Erotic Adventures: Books 31 - 35

Jade's Erotic Adventures: Books 36 - 40

Jade's Erotic Adventures: Books 41 - 45

Jade's Erotic Adventures: Books 46 - 50

Fifty Shades of Jade: Superbundle

Standalone Stories:

The Polynesian Girl: A Lesbian EroticRomance

FOLLOW VICTORIA RUSH:

Want to keep informed of my latest erotic book releases? Sign up for my newsletter and receive a FREE bonus book:

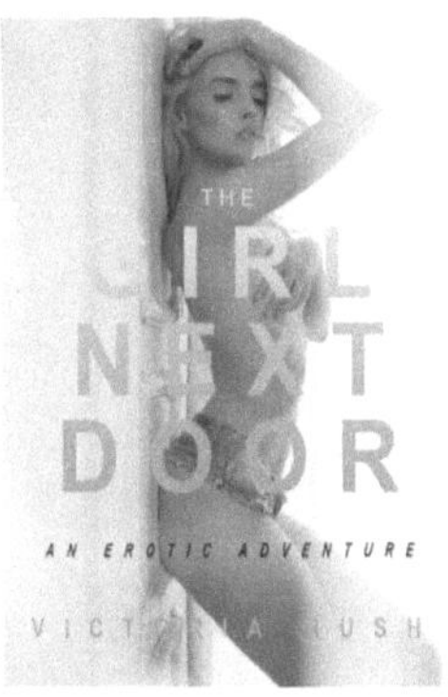

Spying on the neighbors just got a lot more interesting...

www.ingramcontent.com/pod-product-compliance
Lightning Source LLC
Chambersburg PA
CBHW061552310726
48972CB00008B/2721